A History of STRENGTH to Survive and Win!

My sincere thanks to the following people for their time, information, images and enthusiasm for this book:

Joe Saunders, Brisbane, Australia

Katrina Watts, and members of the Australian Sumo Federation, Brisbane, Australia

Adriane Wilson (née Blewitt), Irmo, South Carolina, the USA

Dear Reader

Think about the hundreds of muscles in your body that enable you to move, breathe and keep your blood circulating. About 40 per cent of your body is made up of muscles, and in this book we'll look at some of the main ones that enable us to stay strong and active.

I enjoyed writing about two strength sports: sumo wrestling from Japan and Highland games from Scotland. Today, people from around the world compete in these sports. In Chapter 7, I am delighted to feature Joe Saunders, who is a successful sumo wrestler in Australia. In Chapter 10, you'll meet Adriane Wilson, who is a world champion in Women's Scottish Highland games.

> "WHEN I BEGAN TO COMPETE IN SCOTTISH HIGHLAND GAMES, I TRACKED DOWN MY SCOTTISH HERITAGE TO MY GRANDMOTHER'S ANCESTORS."
>
> ADRIANE WILSON

Take a deep breath, flex your muscles and enjoy the book!

Sharon Parsons

For learning solutions, visit **cengage.com.au**

Contents

A History of STRENGTH to Survive and Win!

1 What Is Strength?

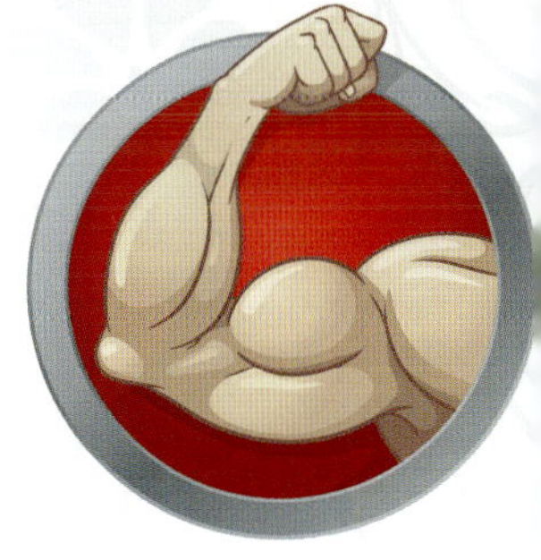

Hypothetical Situations in the **Year 1012**

Strength in Earlier Times

Before the advent of steam-powered machines, people had only their physical and mental strength to perform the tasks required to survive. They were also reliant on the weather. If you could ask a farmer who lived in the year 1012 what strength was, he or she might say, "Strength is being energetic enough to plough my fields, plant my crops and harvest food from dawn to dusk in order to feed my family. I also have to hope that the weather will be good enough to grow sufficient crops to provide enough food this season and for the winter months."

BEFORE Steam-Powered Machines Were Invented

Food: hunt animals, cultivate fields to grow crops, harvest crops

Water: find, collect and carry water home

Tools: find natural materials to make into tools

Shelter: find and fashion materials to build permanent homes and semi-permanent shelters

Transport: walk or run

Before the 1700s, much of the work on a farm (left) was done by hand. Animals were used for harder work, such as ploughing (above). People and animals often lived in the same building (below).

History

The Industrial Revolution

The Industrial Revolution was a significant period in history that began in Great Britain during the 1700s – an era when many inventions helped people to produce goods faster and on a larger scale than before. With the invention of steam-powered engines, people found many uses in manufacturing and transportation. For instance, steam trains made travel and transportation more time-efficient.

Hypothetical Situations in the **Year 2012**

Strength in Modern Times

A thousand years later, if you asked a farmer the same question, he or she might give you an answer like, "Strength is being able to maintain my farm machinery, including lifting and replacing heavy mechanical parts, from plough to harrow to seed planter to harvester. I like to start work at dawn but it isn't necessary these days with farming technology. I check the internet daily to find out the weather forecast and I research the best times to plant crops and the most effective fertilisers to improve crop productivity."

AFTER Steam-Powered Machines Were Invented

Food Option 1: cultivate a garden to plant and grow fruit and vegetables at home

Food Option 2: walk, cycle or drive to the supermarket, farmers' market or fruit and vegetable vendor

an organic vegetable garden in Alsace, France

Supermarket shopping for food saves time.

a farmer in a wheat field during harvest season

Water: water is piped to homes from water tanks and large storage reservoirs

Over 90% of the daily journeys in Hong Kong take place on public transport, which is the highest rate in the world.

Tools: buy tools to do household jobs or hire people with the tools and skills to do the jobs

Shelter: employ skilled tradespeople to build homes

Qualified builders are essential on every building site.

Transport: walk, cycle, drive or catch public transport

Strengthening Muscles for Sports

The **Body's** Main **Muscle** Groups

Different muscle groups are used for all kinds of sports. Today, people want to ensure that they target certain muscles in the body when exercising for general health and wellbeing, or when they're training for particular sports activities. In this chapter, some of the main muscle groups used in sports and training are outlined, including examples of some relevant sports.

Upper Body

The trapezius **muscles span the shoulder and neck, and they enable the arms to raise above shoulder height.**

Lateral raises will strengthen the trapezius *muscles for basketball, baseball and softball.*

Rowing is one exercise that can strengthen the triceps for sports such as rowing, tennis, football, baseball and volleyball.

"Triceps", or triceps brachii**, are found in the upper arm.**

Pull-ups will strengthen the latissimus dorsi *muscles for swimming and tennis.*

"Lats" is short for latissimus dorsi**, which are the widest muscles on either side of the back. These muscles move the shoulders.**

Lower back

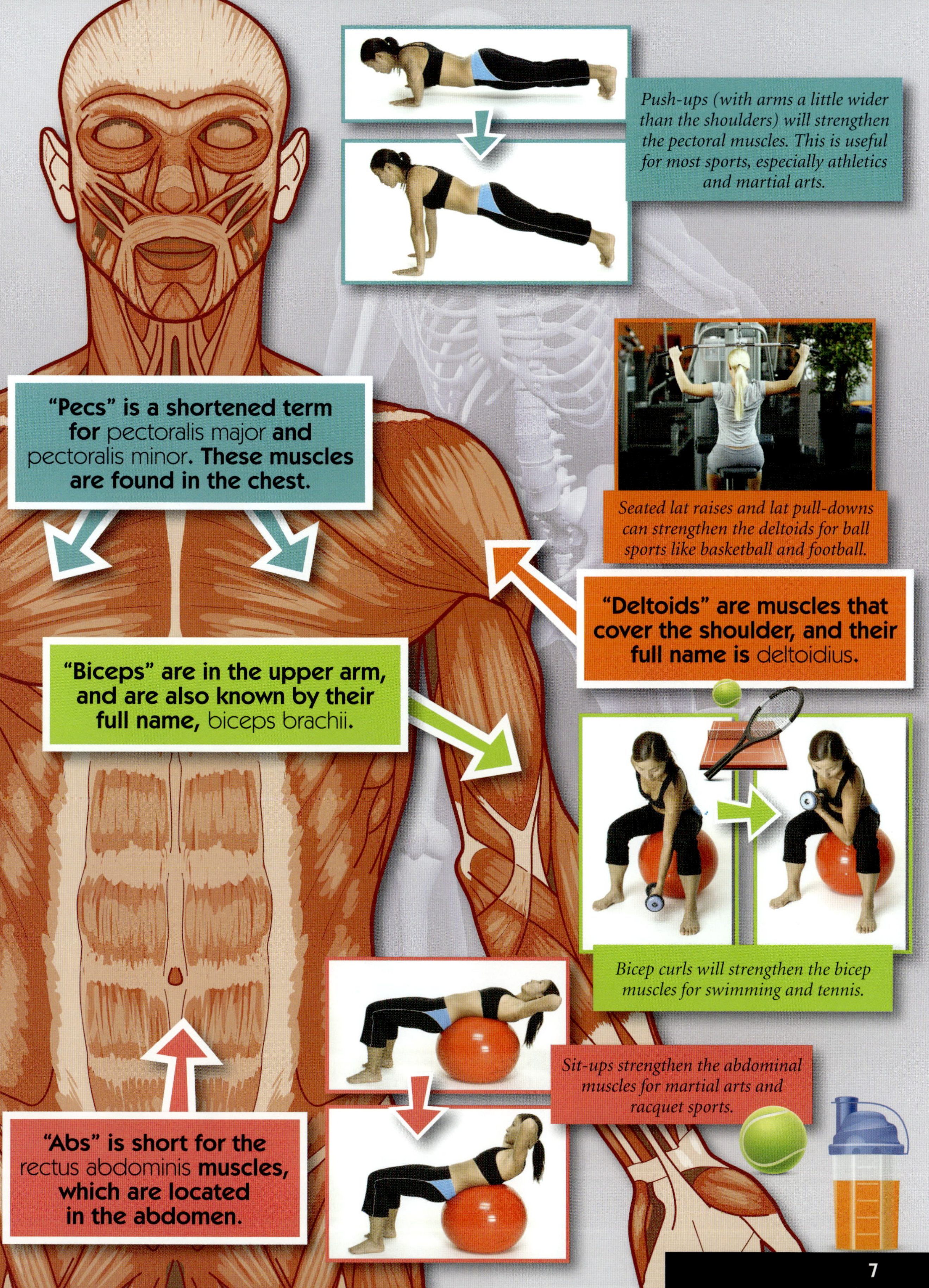
Push-ups (with arms a little wider than the shoulders) will strengthen the pectoral muscles. This is useful for most sports, especially athletics and martial arts.
"Pecs" is a shortened term for pectoralis major and pectoralis minor. These muscles are found in the chest.
Seated lat raises and lat pull-downs can strengthen the deltoids for ball sports like basketball and football.
"Deltoids" are muscles that cover the shoulder, and their full name is deltoidius.
"Biceps" are in the upper arm, and are also known by their full name, biceps brachii.
Bicep curls will strengthen the bicep muscles for swimming and tennis.
Sit-ups strengthen the abdominal muscles for martial arts and racquet sports.
"Abs" is short for the rectus abdominis muscles, which are located in the abdomen.

Lower Body

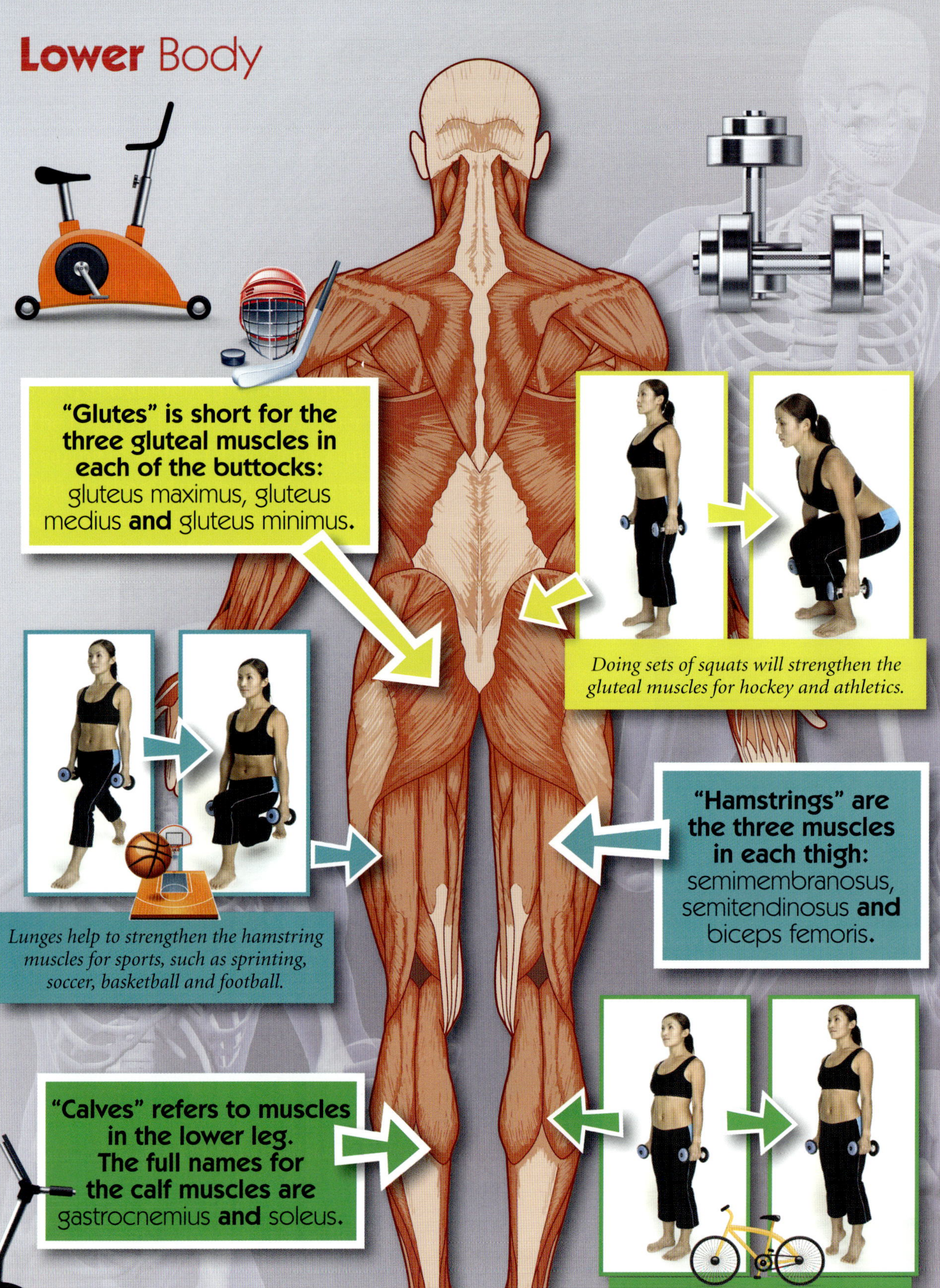

"Glutes" is short for the three gluteal muscles in each of the buttocks: gluteus maximus, gluteus medius **and** gluteus minimus.

Doing sets of squats will strengthen the gluteal muscles for hockey and athletics.

"Hamstrings" are the three muscles in each thigh: semimembranosus, semitendinosus **and** biceps femoris.

Lunges help to strengthen the hamstring muscles for sports, such as sprinting, soccer, basketball and football.

"Calves" refers to muscles in the lower leg. The full names for the calf muscles are gastrocnemius **and** soleus.

Calf raises strengthen the calf muscles for sprinting and cycling.

"Quads" refers to the quadriceps, a group of four muscles in each leg. The anatomical names for the four muscles are vastus medialis, vastus intermedius, vastus lateralis and rectus femoris.

WHY WE NEED STRONG MUSCLES

In the human body, there are 640 muscles that have been identified and named. Keeping these muscles strong helps our overall health and enables us to do a variety of physical activities efficiently. Strong muscles also assist good posture, especially when sitting and standing for long periods of time.

Using an exercise ball for squats against the wall assists quad muscle strength.

Weighted medicine balls help to intensify squat exercises.

Lunges are good exercises to strengthen the quads, which are useful for sports, such as rowing, athletics, martial arts and racquet sports.

3 Sumo, a Strength Sport

JAPAN

Sumo History

Sumo wrestling began about 1 500 years ago, and still continues today as Japan's national sport. In its earliest forms, sumo matches also involved dancing.

Sumo means "the way of the gods", and in early times, sumo was performed to entertain the gods in religious ceremonies.

Today, the sport of sumo is still a traditional way of entertaining the gods in Japan. Usually, men compete in sumo, but on rare occasions women participate in amateur matches.

Rikishi is Japanese for Sumo Wrestler

SUMO IN JAPAN

Every year in Japan, there are six tournaments that each last for 15 days.

Himeno Takashi of Japan and Ulambayer Byambajav of Mongolia wrestle during a sumo competition at the 2010 SportAccord Combat Games in Beijing, China.

Symbols in the Sumo Ring

Sumo wrestling owes its inception to the indigenous Japanese religion, Shinto. There are many symbols in sumo that were derived from Shinto.

a Shinto shrine in Koya-san, Japan (right)

Tassels: Each corner of the canopy has a tassel of a different colour attached, which represents each season – white for autumn, black for winter, green for spring and red for summer.

Canopy: The design of the canopy above the ring resembles the roof of a Shinto shrine.

Bunting: The purple fabric around the roof is a symbol of clouds drifting and the change of seasons.

Sand: The sand used to cover the clay on the sumo *dohyo*, which is the ring in which sumo wrestling bouts are held, is a symbol of purity.

Symbols of Sumo Clothing

String Fringes: Odd numbers of twisted strings are tucked into the sumo wrestler's belt to represent the sacred ropes in front of Shinto temples.

Strips of Paper: A *yokozuna* (the highest level of sumo wrestler) wears a zigzag pattern of white strips of paper on his braided belt to display his high rank. The pattern resembles the arrangements at the entrance to Shinto temples.

(right) Sumo Grand Champion Asashoryu performs dohyo-iri *(a ring purification ritual) at the Meiji Jingu Shrine in Tokyo, Japan.*

SYMBOL OF SALT

Tradition requires a sumo wrestler to toss salt into the ring as a symbol of purification, and to throw salt on his or her body for protection from any evil spirits.

Sumo wrestlers and the judge throw salt in a ceremonial manner onto the dohyo at a Grand Sumo Tournament in Tokyo, Japan.

Rules of Sumo

A sumo wrestling match takes place on a raised platform in a ring called a *dohyo*. The most important rule is that a sumo wrestler will lose the match if they fall over in the ring, or are pushed out of it. The fights usually last a matter of seconds or, on rare occasions, over a minute.

Two sumo wrestlers practise before competing at a Grand Sumo Tournament in Tokyo, Japan.

In Japan, there are no weight restrictions for sumo, so wrestlers aim to gain as much weight as possible in order to get the ultimate advantage over his or her opponent. But, in internationally held sumo championships, competitors are organised in weight divisions – lightweight (men under 85 kilograms), middleweight (men under 115 kilograms) and heavyweight (men over 115 kilograms).

While it is rare in Japan for women to compete in sumo, the international divisions for female sumo competitors are: lightweight (under 65 kilograms), middleweight (under 80 kilograms) and heavyweight (over 80 kilograms).

autumn at the Kinkaku-ji *temple in Kyoto, Japan*

Social Studies

Sumo on Mother's Day

Since 1991, female sumo wrestlers have competed in a sumo competition on Mother's Day in Fukushima, Hokkaido, Japan. The annual event honours two famous sumo wrestlers that were born in their town.

4 Sumo Strength and Balance

Ever wondered how a sumo wrestler weighing over 200 kilograms could have such good balance and ultra-quick reflexes?

Sumo wrestlers train daily to build balance and strength by doing *shiko*, which is a series of leg-stomping exercises. Traditionally in *shiko*, each leg is raised high and wide, then slammed down with great force and balance. Quick hand- and foot-shuffling movements help the sumo wrestler to sharpen his or her reflexes.

Inside a Sumo Stable

The Sumo Stable

Professional sumo wrestlers are usually aged between 20 and 35 years old, and they belong to a stable, which is run by a stable master. A stable is a place where sumo wrestlers live, train and learn the traditions required to compete at the elite level.

5 Sumo Food for Size and Strength

A sumo wrestler has a special diet to build his or her physique and maintain body size. *Chanko* (or *chanko-nabe*) is a Japanese stew that sumo wrestlers eat in large quantities at least twice a day. The ingredients for *chanko-nabe* are high in protein and carbohydrates. Sumo wrestlers gain a lot of weight from eating huge amounts of *chanko-nabe* and, after each meal, it is customary to take a long nap so that the high intake of calories can be stored as fat rather than burned during exercise.

Chanko-Nabe

Traditionally, the recipe for *chanko-nabe* can be made with meat or fish (but not both together) and any kind of vegetable. The ingredients are cooked in a *chanko-nabe* hot pot.

There are many varieties of *chanko-nabe*, but in Japanese sumo culture, the more chicken pieces or chicken balls used, the more good luck the eater will have.

Chicken *Chanko-Nabe*

Chanko made with chicken is served during a sumo tournament as it is considered to bring good luck. One rationale for this belief is that a chicken walks on two legs, and so must a sumo wrestler to remain in the match.

The younger, less experienced sumo wrestlers prepare the food for the chanko-nabe.

CHANKO-NABE

Japanese characters for *chanko-nabe*:

ちゃんこ鍋 / ちゃんこなべ

Recipe for Sumo Stew

Title

A *Chanko-Nabe* Recipe

Goal

To make a dish that is suitable for sumo wrestlers to consume, according to Japanese tradition.

Equipment

- A large stainless-steel pot for cooking
- A large casserole dish for serving
- 2 chopping boards – 1 for chicken and 1 for vegetables
- A large stainless-steel, glass or plastic bowl
- A long-handled, stainless-steel spoon
- A small, sharp knife
- 4 deep soup bowls

Ingredients

- 1 kilogram of chicken thigh fillets
- 1/3 cup of soy sauce
- 1 cup of chicken stock
- 200 grams of fresh tofu
- 200 grams of udon noodles or egg noodles
- 2 teaspoons of salt
- 1/4 medium cabbage
- 2 medium onions
- 3 medium potatoes
- 3 medium carrots
- 6 shiitake mushrooms
- 1 large leek
- 1 daikon radish (optional)

Recipe for sumo stew continues on pages 18–19

Recipe for Sumo Stew

TEXT TYPE
Procedure

Method

Step 1. Cut the onions, potatoes and carrots into bite-sized pieces on the chopping board for vegetables, and set them aside in the large bowl (stainless-steel, glass or plastic).

Step 2. Slice the cabbage, the shiitake mushrooms and the optional ingredient (daikon radish) and add them to the other vegetables.

Step 3. Cut the chicken into chunks (about two centimetres squared) on the chopping board for meat.

Step 4. Add cold water to fill a third of the large stainless-steel pot, and place the pot on the stove on a medium heat.

Step 5. Add the chicken stock, salt and the chopped chicken thigh fillets, to the pot and bring to the boil.

Watch the pot until the liquid is boiling. Then turn the heat down to a low–medium setting to allow the chicken to gently simmer, and give it a quick stir.

Step 6. Simmer for about 30 minutes on a low–medium heat until the chicken is cooked. Use the stainless-steel spoon to stir the mixture for about five seconds.

Step 7. Add the vegetables to the pot.

If you need help, ask an adult to hold the bowl.

Step 8. Add the soy sauce to the vegetables and chicken, and simmer for about 20–30 minutes, until the vegetables are cooked.

Step 9. Chop the tofu into bite-sized cubes and then add to the pot.

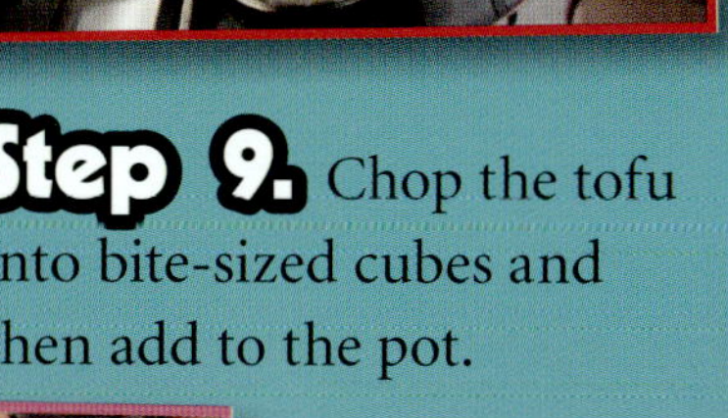

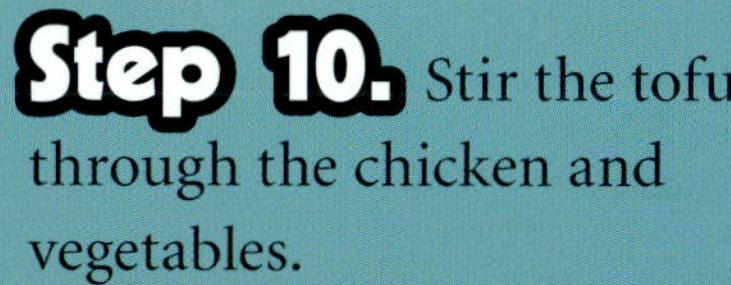

Step 10. Stir the tofu through the chicken and vegetables.

Step 11. Add the noodles and simmer for a further 10 minutes.

This is how the sumo stew looks when it is ready to serve.

Step 12. Serve the sumo stew (*chanko-nabe*) in the soup bowls.

Enjoy!

("Enjoy" is *Tanoshimu* in Japanese.)

7 Sumo in Australia

Sumo wrestling is now an international sport, with over 80 countries belonging to the International Sumo Federation. In 1992, the Australian Sumo Federation was founded, and teams from around the country compete in various international events, such as the World Combat Games.

Joe Saunders (right) competing at the Oceania Sumo Championships in 2010.

Australian Sumo Team Wins Championship

In 2010, the Australian team of six sumo wrestlers won seven medals (two gold, four silver and one bronze) at the Oceania Sumo Championships held in Lower Hutt, New Zealand.

Queensland Sumo Wrestler Wins!

At the 2010 Oceania Sumo Championships, 24-year-old Joe Saunders won two gold medals and one silver medal for the Australian team after only two years in the sport. Joe weighs 115 kilograms, which qualifies him for the middleweight division. He enjoys the dynamic and fast pace of the sport, even though the matches may only last between 10 and 15 seconds! He also competes and coaches in other martial arts codes, such as judo.

Joe Saunders (left) with fellow Australian sumo team members with their individual medals and the championship trophy at the 2010 Oceania Sumo Championships.

Joe (left) trains at the beach with a fellow competitor.

Sumo Strength Training

Joe Saunders trains with heavy weights up to three times every week, either in the gym or on the beach. Working out on the sand at the beach helps to strengthen his leg muscles. Joe has even incorporated activities such as pushing his car along the driveway to improve his strength!

Squats for Strength

To build his hip and upper leg strength, Joe does hundreds of squats, with a difference. Sumo wrestlers need to do many squats in each training session that involve lifting each leg high and wide on the rise up from a squat. Each leg-raising action is followed by a powerful downward stamp of the foot on the surface below. This series of exercises helps to build explosive leg strength and balance, which is essential in sumo wrestling.

SUMO WRESTLERS' SQUATS

Sumo wrestlers in Japan are known to do about 1 200 squats in each training session. That equates to 600 leg lifts per leg – high and wide – before stamping each foot down hard on the surface.

8 Strength in Scottish Highland Games

Think of kilts, bagpipes, Highland dancing and the caber toss, and these iconic images will transport you to any one of the many Scottish Highland games events that occur not only throughout Scotland annually, but in other parts of the world, too. For instance, the Scottish Highland Games attract some of the world's biggest crowds in the USA – the first US Highland Games was held in New York in 1836.

At a Scottish Highland games event, you will witness some of the most amazing displays of strength in sports competitions, set against the sound of Scottish and Gaelic music from pipe bands. You will also see skilful Highland dancers and games for the whole family, such as tug of war!

Scotland

Ireland

UNITED KINGDOM

HIGHLAND GAMES IN SAN FRANCISCO

Since 1866, the Caledonian Club of San Francisco's Gathering and Games has been held to preserve their Scottish traditions. Today, it is the largest Highland games event in the USA.

a sportsman preparing to toss the caber at the Cowal Highland Gathering games in Scotland

a countryside scene at Strathspey Valley, Highlands, Scotland

Origin of the Scottish Highland Games

Is Ireland the home of the Scottish Highland games? Scottish historians believe that the games did indeed have their origins in Ireland from around the year 2000 BCE. In the fourth and fifth centuries, groups of an Irish tribe called the Scotti left Dalriada, Ireland, and settled in Scotland, where they named their new settlement Dalriada, too.

In earlier times, the games were not an organised sports event. Instead, they were activities that followed hunting expeditions called *tainchel*. On these occasions, a successful hunt called for hearty feasts and celebrations. Men from different clans (families of the same descent) competed against one another in activities that tested their strength and courage.

War was also a way of life in early Scottish history. Wars were fought between Scottish clans, and between allied Scottish forces and the English. The strength of the soldiers was vital. Tree trunks were cut down and shaped into cabers, which were tossed by the strongest soldiers. This symbolic test of strength is still one of the most coveted "heavy" events at Scottish Highland games gatherings.

girls competing in Highland dancing at the Isle of Skye Highland Games in Portree, Skye Island, Scotland

a competitor preparing to throw a heavy, smooth stone in the stone-put at the Lochearnhead Games in Scotland

a sportsman about to throw a heavy stone in a weight-for-distance event at the Cowal Highland Gathering games in Scotland

Oldest Scottish Highland Games

Since 1314, the Ceres Highland Games have been held in Scotland. Robert the Bruce, who was king of Scotland in the early fourteenth century, officially awarded Ceres the honour of holding the first free games in recognition of their support during the battle of Bannockburn.

THE KINGDOM OF SCOTLAND

The Kingdom of Scotland was founded in the ninth century.

Scottish Highland Games **Outlawed**, 1746–1782

During a period known as the "The Act of Proscription", which occurred between the years 1746–1782, the then English Government (called the Hanoverian Government) outlawed all Scottish traditions in an attempt to eradicate the Highland clans that opposed English rule. The Highland games and all other expressions of Scottish culture were banned, such as the wearing of tartan-fabric clothes and kilts by civilians, as each tartan weave denoted a different clan. In those days, bagpipes were also banned, as they were considered an instrument of war because their distinctive sounds boosted the morale of the Scottish soldiers. The bagpipes were also a formidable form of communication because tunes that meant "advance" or "retreat" could be heard from several kilometres away, above the sounds of battle.

a statue of King Robert the Bruce in Stirling, Scotland

ROBERT THE BRUCE (1274–1329)

Robert the Bruce is remembered as the "Good King Robert" – the king who fought hard for many and won back Scotland's independence from England in 1328, a year before he died.

CLAN CAMPBELL

The Scottish clan Campbell fought alongside the British Government and helped to defeat the rebel clans, known as the Jacobites. One of the famous battles during that time was the Battle of Culloden, fought at Culloden, Scotland, in 1746.

a monument at the site of the Jacobite defeat near Inverness, Scotland

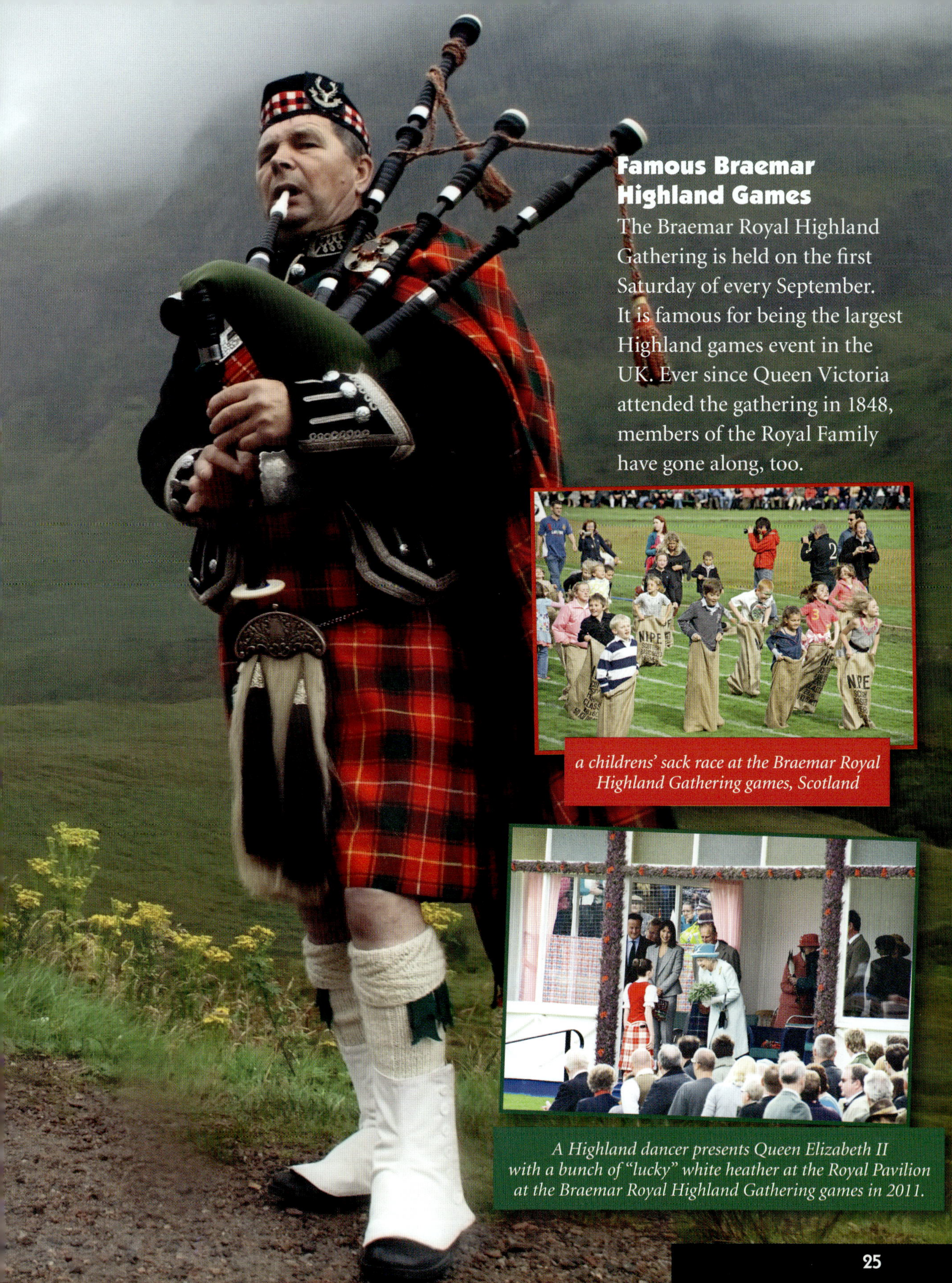

Famous Braemar Highland Games

The Braemar Royal Highland Gathering is held on the first Saturday of every September. It is famous for being the largest Highland games event in the UK. Ever since Queen Victoria attended the gathering in 1848, members of the Royal Family have gone along, too.

a childrens' sack race at the Braemar Royal Highland Gathering games, Scotland

A Highland dancer presents Queen Elizabeth II with a bunch of "lucky" white heather at the Royal Pavilion at the Braemar Royal Highland Gathering games in 2011.

9 Strength Events at Highland Games

A traditional Highland games event is likened to the Scottish Olympics – one key difference is that a competitor cannot choose which of the eight (and sometimes nine) strength or "heavy" events to enter. Every competitor must participate in all eight or nine events.

Official Rules

Official rules are set by the Scottish Highland Games Association. Some of these rules are outlined below for the strength events, which are referred to as "heavy events". The rules and event titles can vary slightly in different parts of the UK and among other countries, too.

At Highland games events, each competitor:

- must wear Highland dress (no exceptions)
- has three attempts at each event to determine their best result (each attempt must not exceed two minutes)
- must compete in every heavy event.

OTHER EVENTS

Other Highland games events include: running, cycling, long jump, triple jump, high jump, pole vault and Scottish professional wrestling.

A competitor exerts his strength and force to throw a 56-pound (or about 25.4-kilogram) weight over a very high bar.

heaving a massive caber in the caber toss event with the utmost strength

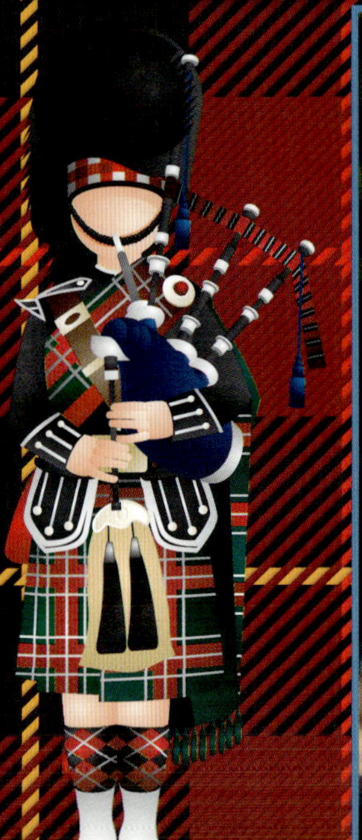

The Twelve O'Clock Caber Toss

The caber toss is not an event based on distance, but rather on strength, balance and accuracy. The event takes place along an imaginary clock face. The competitor usually interlocks his or her hands to hold the tapered end of the caber while resting the beam against the shoulder and neck during the throw. This event relies on strength and balance to hold the long, heavy caber steady while running from the starting spot to reach the desired speed. The point at which the competitor throws the caber becomes the "six o'clock" mark. Then, there is a final forward, heaving motion, so that the heavy end of the caber lands in the middle of the "clock" and topples straight over. Ideally, when the caber falls to the ground, the tapered end should be pointing at the "twelve o'clock" position. It is difficult to achieve a perfect "twelve o'clock" result, so scores can be earned either between the positions of 9.00 and 12.00, or between 12.00 and 3.00.

Rules for Caber Toss

There are no uniform regulations determining the weight or length of the caber, but it must be made of wood and have a tapered end to enable the thrower to rest it in his or her hands. Each Highland games association can determine the weight and length of the caber. At the Braemar Royal Highland Games, the caber's regulation specifications are 59.9 kilograms in weight by six metres in length. One of the heaviest cabers was recorded at 127 kilograms.

ORIGIN OF CABER TOSS

One story handed down is that foresters developed the technique of caber tossing for throwing tree trunks into the river for transportation.

While maintaining balance and momentum, a competitor runs forward to toss the heavy wooden pole in such a way that it turns end over end in the correct caber toss formation.

The Caber Toss

a sportsman releasing the stone in the stone-put event at the Cowal Highland Gathering games in Scotland

Putting the Stone

The stone-put is an event that involves throwing a stone as far as possible. Generally, a participant begins by competing in the lighter 16-pound-stone event (the stone weighs about 7.3 kilograms), and can then choose to progress to the heavier 22-pound-stone event (the stone weighs about 10 kilograms).

The technique is to rest the stone in the hand in front of the shoulder. Then, commence a maximum run of seven-and-a-half feet (about 2.3 metres) before throwing the stone.

Technology

The Trig

The trig is a wooden board that acts as a guide for athletes to use in distance-throwing events, such as the hammer throw. The board is secured into the ground in front of the competitors' throwing box or area.

Highland Games Tug of War Rules

1. Each team can comprise five or eight people, and a coach.

2. A judge tosses a coin to determine the direction that the pull will take.

3. A judge calls out to the teams to first "take the strain," so team members can get ready and dig in their heels. (Footwear may have raised heels of up to seven millimetres.)

4. When the teams are balanced, the judge calls out, "Pull!"

5. All team members' feet must remain on the ground, and competitors cannot put their hands on the ground. Only the "anchor" in the team can put his or her hands on the ground.

6. The pull area is 3.65 metres, and the winning team is the one who wins at least two out of three pulls.

tug of war

More Events at Highland Games

weight-for-distance throw

hammer throw

sheaf toss

Highland dancers competing

weight-for-height throw

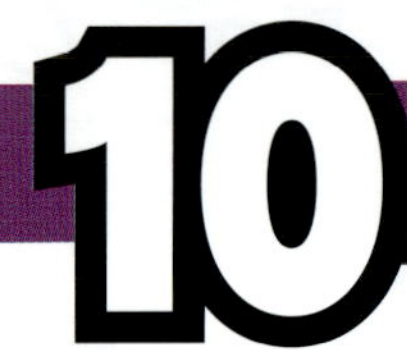

Adriane, World Champion in Heavy Events

Adriane Wilson

In 2010, 2011 and 2012, US athlete Adriane Wilson attained world championship titles at the Women's Scottish Highland Games. Since university, Adriane has excelled at discus, stone-put, javelin and the hammer throw. Adriane's participation in shot-put trials at three Olympic Games helped her to make the transition to the Women's Scottish Highland Games in 2009. The biggest challenge for Adriane was training for nine heavy events, not just two!

Adriane builds up momentum to throw the weight in a weight-for-distance event.

Adriane perfectly balances the pole in the caber toss event.

Scottish Heritage

Adriane proudly says, "When I began to compete in Scottish Highland games, I tracked down my Scottish heritage to my grandmother's ancestors. I am a proud member of Clan MacLeod and wear my tartan when I compete."

Adriane competing in the stone-put

Grip Training

Adriane was able to build her strength through a grip-training program. Adriane explains, " My coach incorporated grip-work into my stone-put training to maintain my hand and wrist health. The constant strain on the wrist and fingers from the release of the stone is tough on throwers. By using a thicker barbell in the bench press, it takes pressure off my elbows and allows me to squeeze the bar with a fuller hand."

Adriane grip training with heavy, thick-handled weights

Adriane's Strength-Training Program

Adriane Wilson follows this training program when she is preparing for a Highland games event. The intensity of the exercises and number of repetitions vary week by week depending on her needs and objectives. Adriane explains, "I focus on strength, speed and technique."

Monday

Running: jog and complete sprints to build cardiovascular fitness and muscular strength.
Throwing: throw lighter and heavier implements for one or two Highland games events.
Strength Training: upper-body weight training and rowing exercises to build strength in the shoulders, triceps and rotator cuffs (groups of muscles and tendons that work to keep the shoulder joints stable).
Grip Training: various exercises using thick-handled dumbbells, handles and barbells for bench pressing.

Tuesday

Running: repeat jogging and sprints workout.
Throwing: throw lighter and heavier implements for one or two Highland games events.
Strength Training: lower-body strength work, including weight-lifting exercises and squats to build strength in the torso, hamstrings, calf muscles and feet.

Wednesday

Rest Day: includes a whole-body massage of the muscles and joints.

Thursday

Running: repeat jogging and sprints workout.
Throwing: throw lighter and heavier implements for one or two Highland games events.
Strength Training: upper-body strength training, including weight-lifting exercises, such as incline dumbbell work, pull-ups and lateral raises.
Grip Training: exercises using thick-handled dumbbells, barbells for bench pressing, and handles of different shapes and sizes to strengthen the grip.

Adriane uses this range of thick-handled dumbbells for grip training.

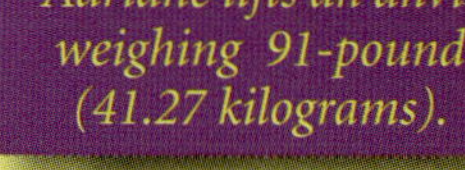

Adriane lifts an anvil weighing 91-pound (41.27 kilograms).

Friday

Running: repeat jogging and sprints workout.
Strength Training: lower-body strength work, including weight-lifting exercises, variations of squats and medicine ball throwing to build strength in the torso, hamstrings, calf muscles and feet.

Saturday

Running: repeat jogging and sprints workout.
Throwing: throw lighter and heavier implements to prepare for the nine Highland games events.

Sunday

Rest Day

Index

Glossary

barbell A piece of equipment used in weight training, made up of a steel bar about two metres long and with disc-shaped weights attached to each end

bench press A weight-training lift where the trainer lies on a bench and lifts a barbell to an arm's length above the chest

caber A large wooden pole that is thrown in a Highland games event called the caber toss

chanko-nabe A Japanese stew often eaten by sumo wrestlers, usually containing meat and vegetables

dohyo The ring in which sumo wrestling matches are held, which is usually covered in sand

dumbbell A piece of equipment used in weight training and usually in pairs, designed to fit in the hand; each dumbbell contains two weights attached to a short handle

lunges Strength training exercises that involve putting one leg forward and bending it at the knee

Shinto The indigenous religion of Japan, which has had a large influence on the sport of sumo wrestling

sprints Exercises that involve running quickly over short distances

yokozuna The highest rank in sumo wrestling